WHENSHEEPCANNOTSLEEP
THE COUNTING BOOK

Satoshi Kitamura

A SUNBURST BOOK • FARRAR, STRAUS AND GIROUX

Special thanks to Alison Sage for her editorial knitting

Copyright © 1986 by Satoshi Kitamura
All rights reserved
Library of Congress catalog card number: 86-45000
Printed in Singapore
First American edition, 1986
Sunburst edition, 1988
Third printing, 1994

One night a sheep called Woolly could not sleep.
"I'll go for a walk," he said, and wandered
off down the meadow.

He chased a butterfly until it flew away
behind a tall green tree.

There on the tree trunk were two ladybirds, fast asleep. "I'm still wide awake," thought Woolly.

"Hoo, hoo, hoo," called the owls.
"Time to go home."

"It's *our* time to come out," said a family of bats,
flittering overhead.

"Apples," said Woolly.
"I knew it was time for something.
   But they are too high up for me."

"Try climbing," said the squirrels.

"Can't," said Woolly.

"There's a ladder," said the squirrels.

They were right.
Woolly put the ladder against the apple tree
and climbed, rung by rung, until he could
reach the sweet, red apples.

It was a lovely calm evening
and Woolly was not a bit sleepy.
Fireflies were dancing in the air . . .

and grasshoppers were singing in the long grass.

Woolly climbed to the top of a hill to look
at the view. Suddenly, flashing lights zipped
across the sky. Woolly was very scared.

He ran as fast as he could to hide amongst the trees, jumping over red tulips as he went.

"What a terrible fright," he panted.
"Where am I?" In front of him was a house
with lots of windows.

The front door was open, so he went in.
There were lots of doors, too.

In one of the rooms, he found some
coloured pencils. "Good," said Woolly.
"I'll do some drawing."

He was so pleased with his pictures
that he hung them on the wall.

"I'm hungry again," said Woolly.
He went into the kitchen and cooked himself
some nice green peas.

He took them into the dining room.
"I'm late for supper," he thought.

"Now for a bath," said Woolly,
"with lots of bubbles."

Next door was a little bed, with a pair
of pyjamas laid neatly on it.
"Stars are out already," thought Woolly.

"Perhaps I'll just lie down . . .
    in case I feel sleepy."

He began to think.

He thought about his mother and his father and
his sisters and brothers and uncles and aunts.
What were they doing? Were they already asleep?
His family and friends went round in his head.
His eyes closed.

Woolly was fast asleep.

INDEX